MOLLY
& THE TIP TOPS

by
Michelle Benjamin

MOLLY
& THE TIP TOPS

First published in Great Britain as a softback original in 2021

Copyright © Michelle Benjamin

The moral right of this author has been asserted.

Typeset in New Century Schoolbook

Editing, design, typesetting and publishing by
UK Book Publishing

www.ukbookpublishing.com

ISBN: 978-1-914195-90-7

CHAPTER 1:
The surprise at the bottom of the garden.

olly lived in a pretty little cottage by the sea with her cat Basil. Molly's home looked like a beautiful picture postcard. Trailing wisteria grew up around the front door, lavender edged the garden path and the most beautiful sweet-smelling roses danced in the breeze.

Molly took great pride in her garden. Molly particularly loved the beautiful magnolia tree that stood majestically at the bottom of the back garden. When it flowered in spring it was an awesome sight. It provided shade for her in the summer months. Molly felt calm when she sat under the tree in her favourite garden chair with Basil at her feet.

Molly loved to get lost in a book with a cup of tea before she started work for the day. Basil was happy to just laze around with Molly by the tree; he was getting old and did not like to move much anymore.

Molly was an author so consequently spent a lot of time in her study writing. Her study window looked out over the back garden towards the magnolia tree. The view gave Molly peace and tranquillity and helped her to focus on her writing.

However, one hot summer's day her life would change forever. Molly would have no idea of the events that were about to unfold in her life.

Molly's alarm went off at six – that was the time Molly got up every morning. She always liked to take her time before she got started on her writing for the day. Molly did not like to be rushed; it made her feel uneasy.

Basil was downstairs as usual waiting by his food bowl to be fed.

"Morning Basil, what a beautiful morning," she said as she poured food into Basil's bowl.

Basil gave a purr and proceeded to

eat. Molly made herself a cup of tea in her favourite mug as she always did in the morning. She opened the windows. It was a particularly hot summer's day and she could smell the sea lingering in the breeze. Molly only had to walk a short distance to the beach. She felt very blessed to be living there. She decided to go to her spot under the magnolia tree and enjoy her cup of tea before she started her writing for the day.

"Are you coming, Basil?" she said.

Basil followed slowly behind and planted himself by Molly's feet as she sipped her tea in her favourite garden chair. She was admiring the array of blooms in her garden. They looked and smelt amazing today. She could hear the water trickling in the distance from the water feature.

"I love the sound of water," she thought to herself.

Suddenly Basil jumped to his feet (which was unusual for him these days) and looked behind the magnolia tree.

"What's up, Basil?" Molly enquired. "What are you looking at?"

Basil was frozen to the ground just staring behind the tree.

"Have you found another frog again?" she questioned.

Frogs frequented Molly's garden quite a lot.

Molly got up from her chair and went to see what Basil was looking at, but as she bent down to investigate further she thought she might faint.

Were her eyes playing tricks on her,

she thought.

"Whatever could this be?"

With her head in a spin she leaned forward and picked up Tommy Tiptop!

Tommy was a Tiptop who lived in the trunk of the magnolia tree and as far as he was concerned no human eye could see him.

Tommy was six inches tall with long spindly arms and legs, and tiny hands and feet. He had wings with all the colours of the rainbow that glistened in the sunlight. His ears were pixie-like and he had the brightest green eyes you ever did see. He wore a waistcoat and trousers of sequins. He shone like the sun.

"Oh my," Molly exclaimed. "What or who on earth are you?"

Molly could not believe her eyes.

Tommy lifted his little head and looked at Molly with his big green eyes and whispered,

"I am Tommy Tiptop, but how can you see me? Humans cannot see me or my kind."

"Do not be frightened, Tommy, I would never hurt you."

Tommy began to feel a little less tense and relax a little.

"You are the most beautiful thing I have ever seen," Molly gasped. "Where do you come from Tommy?"

"I, we that is, live in the magnolia tree, that is our home."

Molly was confused and elated all at the same time.

What on earth would she do with this

knowledge, she thought to herself.

Molly had always loved stories of fairies and pixies and such like, but that is what she thought they were – just stories – up until now.

"A magical creature living in my magnolia tree!" She could hardly contain her excitement.

"How can you see me – we are unseen by the human eye?" Tommy questioned.

"I have no idea, no idea whatsoever," she explained.

Tommy became worried because it wasn't just him who lived in the tree – he had family and friends there also. He started to feel anxious and tense again; he had no idea what Molly's intentions were. He had never spoken to a human before.

Basil lay fixated on the events that were unfolding. His head moving backwards and forwards, listening to the conversation between Molly and Tommy.

"What will you do with me now?" Tommy was scared.

"Why, nothing, my little winged friend, you are safe living in my garden, my lips are sealed."

Tommy felt relieved but still confused and worried that she could see him because if she could see him that meant she could see the rest of them.

"I need to get back home, Molly," Tommy said.

"I need to tell my sister about you. Promise you will come back, Tommy, please promise."

"I will, of course, but for now I have to

go," he replied.

Molly knelt down and put Tommy on the ground ever so gently; she was mindful that he was a delicate creature and she did not want to hurt him.

Tommy ran off as fast as his little legs could carry him back into the trunk of the magnolia tree.

Basil jumped up ready to chase but Molly picked him up and scolded him.

"Oh no you don't, Basil, you be gentle with him."

Molly was left feeling bewildered. She sat and went through the events in her head and then realised as she looked up at the clock that two hours had passed.

Tommy arrived back at his house in the magnolia tree and after closing the door sat down on the floor exhausted.

"What am I to do, what am I to do?" The thought went over and over in his head. No answer came.

Tommy felt deep down that Molly wouldn't tell anyone, but how would he explain it to his friends and family? They would surely be terrified when they knew that a human being could see them.

Tommy heard a knock at the door. He was startled. Tommy opened the door and his sister Mishy Mop was standing there.

"Hi Tommy," she said as she entered the nook. Tip Tops' homes were called nooks by the way.

"Hey," Tommy replied.

"Mum said she is doing lunch tomorrow afternoon and wants us both to come. Dad is talking about building a pond in the garden again, you know how he gets; I think she wants us to try and talk him out of it!" She laughed.

"Ok fine," he replied.

"But Mishy, there is something I have to tell you, but whatever I am about to tell you, you must promise to keep it a secret – do you promise?"

Mishy Mop became concerned when she saw the worried look on Tommy's face.

"Ok, of course, not a word."

"I was in the garden today, you know, the garden of the human..." he began.

"Yes?" Mishy replied.

"Well I'm sorry to say she saw me!!" he exclaimed.

Mishy covered her face with her hands and gasped.

"Are you kidding me!" she shouted. "No way, I mean are you sure?"

"Yes, Mishy, I am sure," Tommy responded. "We had a conversation, and her name is Molly and she has a cat called Basil."

"Oh me, oh my, whatever are we to do?" Mishy replied.

Tommy explained to Mishy that she wasn't to worry or be afraid because Molly had assured him that she would never tell anyone.

"But how can you be sure?" said Mishy.

"I just know I trust her, and she is kind and lovely and you will love her too, Mishy Mop."

"Ok but we should not tell anyone yet, at least not until I meet her myself and decide if she is to be trusted or not."

"Fine, we will go tomorrow at my normal time to the garden," said Tommy. "Molly will be there in her favourite chair in the garden."

"Right, that's it then, I will come in the morning and we will go see this Molly person," said Mishy Mop.

Mishy Mop did not have the same trusting nature as Tommy did, she felt that Tommy was way too trusting and should never have spoken to Molly, but she never told him that.

"I will see you tomorrow then, Mishy Mop, but remember: TELL NO ONE!"

Mishy Mop left and headed for home.

Tommy spent the rest of the day pondering the events that had taken place, and before he knew it dinner time was upon him. Tommy fixed himself some nuts and seeds and prepared himself for bed. He felt extremely nervous about what would unfold tomorrow when Mishy Mop met Molly. After what seemed like an eternity Tommy fell asleep.

16

CHAPTER 2:
We meet again

Tommy had barely opened his eyes when he heard Mishy Mop knocking at his door. Tommy opened the door, in his pyjamas.

"Why are you not dressed, Tommy?" Mishy Mop asked. Mishy Mop could be quite bossy and Tommy sensed annoyance in her voice. "I hardly slept a wink last night and I am so nervous. Come on then, jump to it, get dressed."

Tommy quickly put on his trousers

and waistcoat and they both slid down the trunk of the magnolia tree to Molly's garden.

Molly hadn't slept much either, she had tossed and turned all night wondering if she would ever see Tommy again. Sunlight was flooding through the curtains and she became aware that she had not written any of her book yesterday. She would surely have to catch up today. Molly washed and dressed and went downstairs for her morning cup of tea and to feed Basil. Sure enough, Basil was sitting by his bowl waiting to be fed. Molly filled Basil's bowl and made herself a cup of tea. The sun was shining and Molly could smell the sea on the breeze that was blowing through the window. Molly went out into the garden to sit in her favourite chair underneath the magnolia tree, all the while hoping that she would see her little friend Tommy again today.

Tommy and Mishy Mop were hiding behind the magnolia tree when Tommy turned to Mishy Mop and said, "She's in her chair, Molly is in her chair." The pair crept ever so gently from behind the magnolia tree and sure enough Basil's ears pricked up and he jumped to his feet. Molly knew at that moment it must be Tommy. She got up from her chair and knelt down in the grass. What she had not bargained for is that there would be two of them.

"Why hello there, my little friend." Molly smiled.

"Hello Molly, I would like you to meet

my sister, Mishy Mop."

Molly gently picked up Tommy and Mishy Mop in her hand. "Hello Mishy Mop, ever so pleased to meet you," said Molly.

"Hello," said Mishy Mop hesitantly. Tommy had not seen Mishy Mop so quiet before, she was ever so feisty at times.

"Why, you are ever so beautiful," said Molly.

Mishy Mop smiled and blushed. "Thank you," said Mishy Mop.

"I am so glad you came back, Tommy, I was afraid you wouldn't," said Molly.

Tommy explained to Molly about the fear of Molly telling others about them and how it would endanger him and his family.

"Please, please don't fret, I would

never do such a terrible thing, I will protect you always."

Tommy and Mishy Mop relaxed a little and began to feel a little more comfortable with Molly. Molly sat and chatted with Tommy and Mishy Mop for an hour. They told her of the nooks that they lived in and about their family and friends who lived in the magnolia tree. Tommy and Mishy Mop talked of their mum Lishy and their dad Doddie. They told Molly that they had always lived in the magnolia tree and that every Magnolia tree had a Tip Top family living in it. Molly was fascinated with the conversation. Tommy and Mishy Mop's wings were glistening in the sun and their sequined little outfits shone like the stars.

"We are having lunch with our mum and dad real soon but we are going to keep you a secret for now; Mum can get quite nervous so best to keep it from her," said Mishy Mop.

"Yes I agree," said Tommy.

"Of course, I totally understand," said Molly. "Maybe if you come back tomorrow you might want to visit inside my home?"

"That would be lovely," they both said in unison. Molly lowered Tommy and Mishy Mop to the ground and they waved goodbye as they disappeared behind the magnolia tree. Basil stayed in the kitchen this time; it was all way too much for him to be dealing with.

Molly went back inside to continue her writing and catch up on the missed work from yesterday.

CHAPTER 3:
The well
kept secret

ommy and Mishy Mop hurried up
the trunk of the magnolia tree and
walked briskly to Mummy Lishy
and Daddy Doddie's house. The door
was open when they arrived. Lishy and
Doddie were busy preparing lunch.

"Hello my little pumpkins," said
Mummy Lishy with a huge smile on her
face. She missed her children since they

had moved out.

"Hi Mum, hi Dad," answered
Mishy Mop.

"Hi," said Tommy. They both gave
each other a look and they both knew
what that look meant: 'NOT A WORD
ABOUT MOLLY'

They all sat down for lunch and
sure enough Daddy Doddie told them
all about his idea of building a pond in
the garden. Daddy Doddie was always
planning to make something. Everyone
rolled their eyes.

"Here we go again," said
Mummy Lishy.

"Not sure that is such a good idea,"
said Mishy Mop.

They all knew it didn't matter what
they said, he was going to build it

anyway. Tommy and Mishy Mop said their goodbyes after lunch and needed to get chores done at home. Mummy Lishy always hated it when they left but she waved them goodbye until the next time. They reached Mishy Mop's house first and Tommy reminded her that they were to meet tomorrow and go down to the garden to see Molly.

"I am ever so excited to see what a human's house looks like," announced Tommy.

"Yes, me too, I am so excited I can barely contain myself," said Mishy Mop.

"Okay, see you tomorrow then, Mishy Mop."

"Yes, definitely," she replied.

Tommy did some cleaning and decided that he would get an early night. After all, he hadn't slept much the night before and if he was totally honest he wasn't entirely sure he would get any tonight either. He switched off his lamp and lay down in his comfy little bed. He always loved evening time when he could relax in his cosy bedroom.

Mishy did some chores and decided that she should water her plants in the garden. Mishy Mop loved her flowers, she took great care of them. She got herself ready for bed, but she was way too excited to sleep so she lay in bed and read for a while. Reading helped Mishy Mop to sleep and tonight it worked like a charm, she was asleep in no time.

Molly had finished her writing for the day and she couldn't wait to bring Tommy and Mishy Mop to her home.

She was very house proud and she couldn't possibly go to bed without giving the house a thorough clean and making it smell fresh. Molly would be so totally horrified if visitors came to her house and it was messy. She dusted and polished and vacuumed until it was spick and span. When she was satisfied that everything was up to standard, she got herself ready for bed. Molly tossed and turned for what seemed like forever when she finally drifted off to sleep. No doubt they were all dreaming about their big day tomorrow.

CHAPTER 4:
Molly's home

Sure enough morning came and the sun was shining through Molly's window. Molly was very keen to get out of bed this morning. She was eagerly anticipating her little visitors. Molly got washed and dressed and went downstairs to make her cup of tea and to feed Basil.

Tommy also awoke to the sun streaming through the window and as soon as his eyes opened the excitement and anticipation began. Tommy decided to get ready before Mishy Mop arrived. If he was not dressed she would surely have something to say. Mishy Mop liked everyone to be on time. She was not a fan of lateness.

Mishy Mop had been awake for a very long time but she had lain in bed for a while until it was time for her to get ready. After a while Mishy Mop got herself washed and dressed and walked the short distance to Tommy's house. She was feeling butterflies in her stomach – after all, it wasn't every day in the life of a Tip Top that you got to see inside a human being's house.

Tommy was sitting at the kitchen table when he heard Mishy Mop knocking at the door. Tommy opened

the door and greeted Mishy Mop.
"Morning," he said.

"Morning, Tommy, are you ready?"

"I am indeed, let's go," he replied.

Mishy Mop and Tommy took the short
walk to the bottom of the magnolia
tree and sitting in her chair was Molly
waiting for their arrival.

Basil did his usual jumping to his
feet with his ears pointing upwards as
he heard Mishy Mop and Tommy in the
grass. Molly knew that was her cue to
get her little winged friends.

"Good morning," squealed Molly with
excitement.

"Morning Molly," they both replied.

Molly knelt down and picked up
Tommy and Mishy Mop in the palm of
her hand and walked back down the

garden to the house. Molly stepped into the conservatory and through the hall to the kitchen. Tommy and Mishy Mop commented on how delightful the house smelt and how inviting it was. Molly loved her cottage kitchen; she placed every ornament in just the right places and always had a vase of freshly cut flowers on the island in the centre. Molly had a great eye for detail and her cottage reflected that. Molly placed Tommy and Mishy Mop on the kitchen table and sat down beside them.

"So, my little friends," said Molly, "what do you think so far?"

Mishy Mop, who also prided herself on keeping a clean and tidy house replied, "Molly this is the most beautiful, sweet smelling house I have ever seen."

"What about you, Tommy, what do you think?"

"It is truly wonderful here, Molly, you must truly love this place," he replied.

Molly smiled; it was certainly true. She loved her home. It was her peaceful little haven.

Molly took them both into every room in the cottage. She explained her reasons behind every paint colour and soft furnishing to every picture that hung on the walls. Mishy Mop became particularly fond of a brightly coloured shell that sat on the bathroom windowsill.

"I love that shell, Molly, it is very beautiful," said Mishy Mop.

"It is indeed but you can have it for your home, a little present from me to you," said Molly.

"I can? Wow, thank you, Molly, thank you ever so much."

Tommy rolled his eyes, Mishy Mop always seemed to get things for free. Everywhere she went she came away with something.

Tommy and Mishy Mop became aware that they should get back home before anyone realised that they were missing. "We really should go, Molly we will be missed at home," said Tommy.

"Okay, that's fine, but when will I see you again?"

Tommy and Mishy Mop looked at each other and were both thinking the same thing. Tommy turned to Mishy Mop and said, "Mishy Mop, what do you think about Molly coming to our home and meeting our family?"

"I think that is a fabulous idea but we need to talk to Mum and Dad about Molly and give them warning," she said.

"But I wouldn't fit in your home," said Molly.

"Well, we have special dust that can make things smaller, Molly, but it only lasts one hour. We would have to make sure that you were out of the tree before the hour is up," said Mishy Mop.

"That sounds amazing, you let me know when you have spoken to your mum and dad and I will be ready."

Tommy and Mishy Mop said that they would tomorrow and all being well Molly could visit the day after. Molly promised to meet them at the bottom of the tree in two days' time. Tommy and Mishy Mop proceeded to home in the magnolia tree.

36

CHAPTER 5:
The secret
revealed

ommy and Mishy Mop went back to Mishy Mop's house to talk about how they would break the news about Molly to their parents. They sat at the kitchen table with some berry water and proceeded to discuss events.

"When do you think is the best time to tell Mum and Dad, because realistically we only have one day to prepare them," said Tommy.

"Hmmm, it's tricky, isn't it, because you know how Mum gets when she's stressed. Dad will take it calmer for sure," said Mishy Mop.

"Maybe we should invite them to lunch tomorrow and share the news then," said Tommy.

"Yes, great idea, let's do that and I will see you tomorrow."

Mishy Mop left and walked the short distance to Mummy Lishy and Daddy Doddie's house. Mummy Lishy was in the garden watering plants and Dad was sat in his chair, reading. They were both surprised to see her – Mishy Mop never said she was coming over today.

"Hi Mum, hi Dad," she said. "Tommy and me want to invite you for lunch at

Tommy's house tomorrow, are you free?"

"That sounds fabulous, Mishy Mop, it will be nice to have someone else do the cooking for a change," Mummy Lishy replied.

"Yes, that's a lovely idea, thank you," said Daddy Doddie.

"Great, I will come and pick you up tomorrow at around 11.45, bye for now," and off she went.

Mishy Mop went home and did some chores and relaxed with a book for the afternoon. Tommy went to visit a friend; he had not been out much the last few days.

Molly spent the rest of the day catching up with her writing; after all, she had lots to do.

The next day Mishy Mop went to

collect her parents and they walked down to Tommy's house together. Tommy had prepared berry water and nut casserole.

"Smells amazing," said Mummy Lishy.

They all sat down at the kitchen table and had lunch together. Everyone commented on how lovely the meal was.

"Erm, Mum, Dad, me and Mishy Mop have something to tell you," said Tommy.

Mummy Lishy and Daddy Doddie looked at each other and looked at their two children.

Tommy blurted out, "We have met the human in the garden, her name is Molly and she can see us."

Everyone was silent for a few seconds. Mishy Mop felt uneasy with the awkward silence.

"How on earth, Tommy, why would you think it is okay to talk to a human? Besides, humans are not supposed to be able to see us!" Mummy Lishy got up from the table and started to pace the floor.

"Calm down, now, Mummy Lishy, calm down," said Daddy Doddie. Daddy Doddie questioned Tommy and Mishy Mop about how they came to meet Molly while Mummy Lishy sat in silence.

On listening to the conversation and hearing how lovely and kind Molly was, Mummy Lishy calmed down a little. "So what now then?" said Mummy Lishy.

"Well we thought that it would be a good idea for Molly to come here and meet us," said Mishy Mop.

"But that means we will have to

use the special shrinking dust and
you know it only lasts one hour," said
Daddy Doddie.

"Yes, we know and we have told
Molly this. She is very excited to come
here and I just know you will love her,"
said Tommy.

"Okay then," both parents agreed.

"Great, we will bring her here
tomorrow," said Mishy Mop.

"I am not entirely happy about this
but we will see," said Mummy Lishy as
she was leaving.

Tommy and Mishy Mop sat down at
the kitchen table with a sigh of relief.
They both knew it could have been
much worse.

"Well, I am glad that is over,"
said Tommy.

"Indeed, me too," said Mishy Mop.

Mishy Mop said goodbye to Tommy and promised to meet him tomorrow with the shrinking dust to meet Molly. He waved her off and decided to have a lie down. It was all a little too much excitement for one day.

Daddy Doddie was excited about tomorrow. Mummy Lishy was not!

CHAPTER 6
Hello Molly

The sun shone through Molly's window and she could hear birdsong. She quickly jumped out of bed as she came to the realisation that today was the day. The day when she got to go to Tommy's house and meet his family. Molly quickly got washed and dressed. She went downstairs, fed Basil and made herself a cup of tea. She carried her tea into the garden and sat in her favourite chair, waiting patiently for Tommy and Mishy Mop to arrive.

Tommy woke from his sleep and stumbled out of bed for some berry juice. All he could think about was the fact that Molly would be meeting his parents today. Oh, how he hoped everything would be okay.

Mishy Mop woke to the sound of her alarm. She jumped out of bed and checked to make sure the shrinking dust was still where she had left it in the cupboard. She then proceeded to get washed and dressed. She grabbed a few nuts and seeds and with the shrinking dust in hand she walked the short distance to Tommy's house.

Mishy Mop knocked at the door. Tommy opened the door and greeted Mishy Mop and they both made their way down the trunk of the magnolia tree into Molly's garden. Sure enough, they found Molly in her usual place.

"Morning, Molly, are you ready?" asked Tommy.

"Oh yes, I am indeed, I am just so excited!"

Mishy Mop took out the shrinking dust. "Now remember, Molly, we only have one hour before the shrinking dust wears off so we have to be quick."

"Of course, yes," said Molly. Mishy threw the dust over Molly and instantly she had shrunk to the size of Tommy and Mishy Mop. Molly was beyond herself with excitement.

"Come on, quick, let's go," said Tommy.

All three climbed inside the trunk of the magnolia tree and through the door to Tommy's world.

"Wow," said Molly as she entered. "This is truly unbelievable, a whole new world in here right in my garden."

Molly gazed in awe at all the little nooks and gardens where the Tip Tops lived. She could not believe what she was seeing. Tommy was eager to get to his parents' house so he hurried them along. Mishy Mop knocked at Daddy Doddie and Mummy Lishy's door. Daddy Doddie opened the door.

"Well, hello there," said Daddy Doddie, "so pleased to meet you."

"Very pleased to meet you too," said Molly.

Mummy Lishy came to the door looking a little cautious. "Hello Molly," she said.

"Hello, so very nice to meet you,"
Molly replied.

They all sat down at the kitchen table
and Molly told them all about her world.
Her home, her cat and her garden. Time
passed quickly. It was time to leave
before the shrinking dust wore off. They
said their goodbyes and headed quickly
towards the trunk.

"Come on, quickly, Molly, we are
running out of time," said Tommy.

"Okay okay," said Molly.

Finally they arrived safely back in
Molly's garden and no sooner was she
there she could feel the dust wearing off,
she was getting back to her normal self.

"Wow, that was close," said Mishy Mop

"Too close if you ask me," said Tommy.

All three sat down and talked about

the visit to the magnolia tree.

"When can I go back again?"
asked Molly.

"Well, we will have to see because we
cannot afford for you to be seen by others
just yet," said Tommy.

"Of course, I can understand that, but
what about your mum and dad coming to
my house then?" asked Molly.

"I will talk to them about that," said
Tommy. "We should go now, Molly,
but we will be back tomorrow," said
Mishy Mop.

"See you tomorrow then," she said.

Tommy and Mishy Mop left to go
home and Molly sat in her chair. Molly
looked down and saw that something
was in the grass. Molly leaned down and
picked it up. "Oh my, it's the shrinking

dust," she said.

Molly would return the dust to Tommy tomorrow, but she just could not wait for her next adventure. Who would she meet in Tip Top land next, she thought. Her life would never be the same again – she had so many adventures in store.

Printed in Great Britain
by Amazon

11281967R00032